This book belongs to:

Elin Opthus

Disney PRINCESS

THE Little Mermaid

The Story of Ariel

Disney PRINCESS

THE Little Mermaid

The Story of Ariel

Disney PRESS

Los Angeles • New York

Published by Disney Press, an imprint of Disney Book Group. No part of this book may be reproduced or transmitted in any form or by any means, electronic or mechanical, including photocopying, recording, or by any information storage and retrieval system, without written permission from the publisher. For information address Disney Press, 1101 Flower Street, Glendale, California 91201.

Printed in the United States of America
First Hardcover Edition, January 2016
1 3 5 7 9 10 8 6 4 2

Library of Congress Control Number: 2015947452
FAC-038091-15324
ISBN 978-1-4847-6728-3

disneybooks.com

SUSTAINABLE FORESTRY INITIATIVE Certified Sourcing
www.sfiprogram.org
SFI-00993
This Label Applies to Text Stock Only

Explore new worlds . . .

DEEP UNDER THE SEA, the merfolk and sea creatures hurried to King Triton's glittering palace. Ariel, his youngest daughter, was making her musical debut in a special concert, and no one wanted to miss a single note.

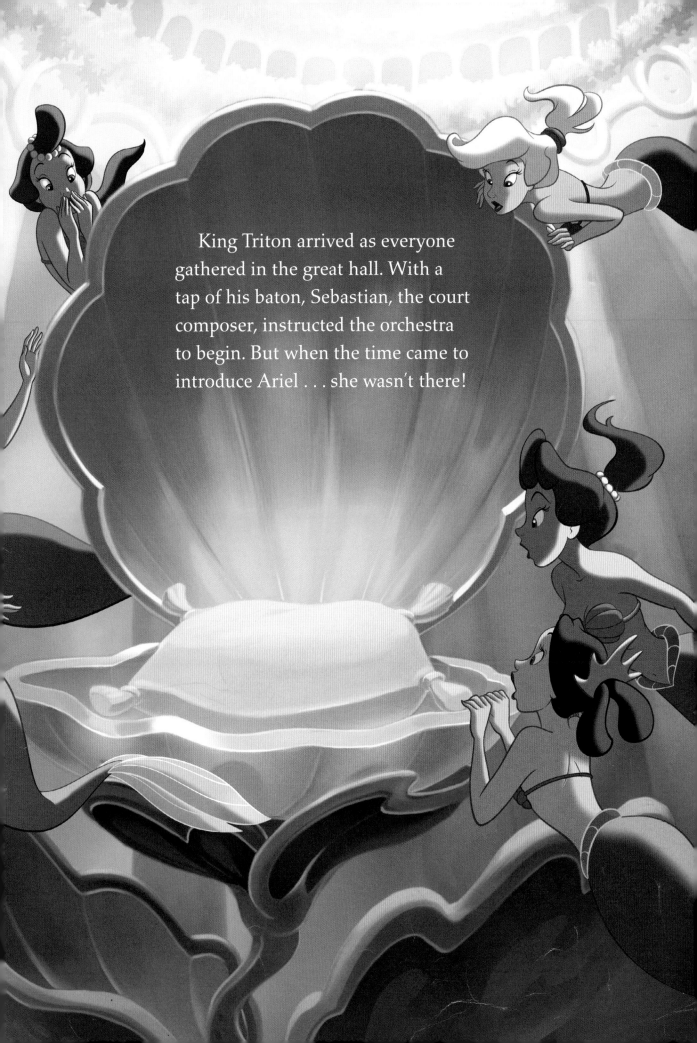

King Triton arrived as everyone gathered in the great hall. With a tap of his baton, Sebastian, the court composer, instructed the orchestra to begin. But when the time came to introduce Ariel . . . she wasn't there!

Ariel had forgotten about the concert. She was miles away, searching for human treasures. In the murky depths, she hurried toward a sunken ship. "Isn't it fantastic?" Ariel exclaimed to her friend Flounder.

Flounder nervously followed Ariel into the ship.

"Have you ever seen anything so wonderful in your entire life?" Ariel asked, picking up a silver fork.

"Yeah, it's great," Flounder said. "Now let's get out of here."

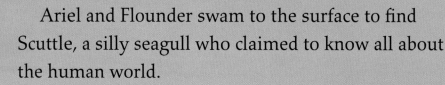

Ariel and Flounder swam to the surface to find Scuttle, a silly seagull who claimed to know all about the human world.

Scuttle examined the fork. "It's a dinglehopper," he said. "Humans use these little babies to straighten their hair out."

Just then, Ariel remembered the concert. "My father's gonna kill me!" she said.

In her cavern, Ursula the sea witch used her magic to watch Ariel hurry home. "She may be the key to Triton's undoing," Ursula said with an evil smile.

When King Triton learned from Sebastian that Ariel had missed the concert because she had been to the surface, he was furious. He believed humans were dangerous, and he wanted to protect her. "You are never to go to the surface again!" he commanded.

The king asked Sebastian to keep an eye on Ariel, so he followed Ariel and Flounder to a secret grotto. He was stunned to see it was filled with human treasures. Horrified, the little crab listened to Ariel tell Flounder how much she wanted to be part of the human world.

Sebastian tried to talk some sense into Ariel, but she wasn't listening. Before he could stop her, Ariel swam to the surface again—to watch a ship that was sailing past.

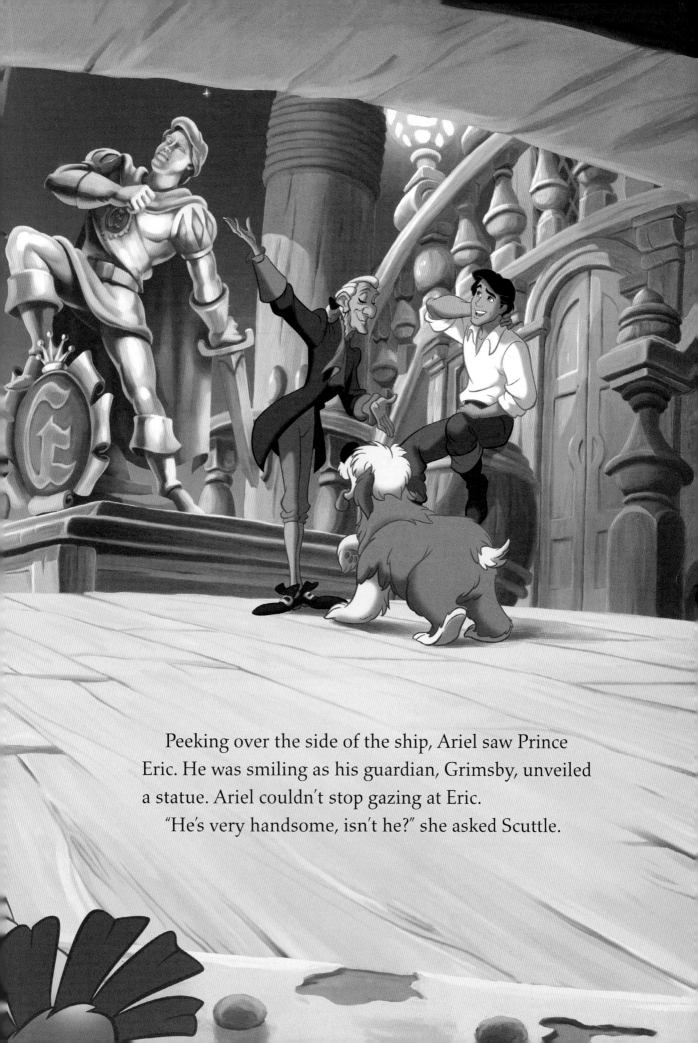

Peeking over the side of the ship, Ariel saw Prince
Eric. He was smiling as his guardian, Grimsby, unveiled
a statue. Ariel couldn't stop gazing at Eric.
"He's very handsome, isn't he?" she asked Scuttle.

Ariel noticed dark clouds gathering over the ship. In an instant, thunder roared and lightning crackled. A lightning bolt lit the ship on fire. Huge waves swept Eric into the sea.

Beneath the waves, Ariel grasped
the unconscious prince in her arms.
Struggling through the fierce current,
she pulled him to safety.

Ariel sang in a beautiful voice about her hopes to be a part of his world. The sound of humans approaching made her dive quickly into the sea. Eric caught only a glimpse of Ariel's face, but he had heard her singing. He would remember her voice forever.

The next day, Ariel swam around in a daze, plucking sea flowers and humming softly. All she could think about was being on land with Prince Eric. Her strange behavior caught King Triton by surprise. He assumed she was in love and questioned Sebastian about it.

Sebastian led King Triton to Ariel.
At the entrance to her grotto, Triton
watched Ariel sing and talk to the
statue of Eric that had fallen from the
ship. Her father exploded in rage.

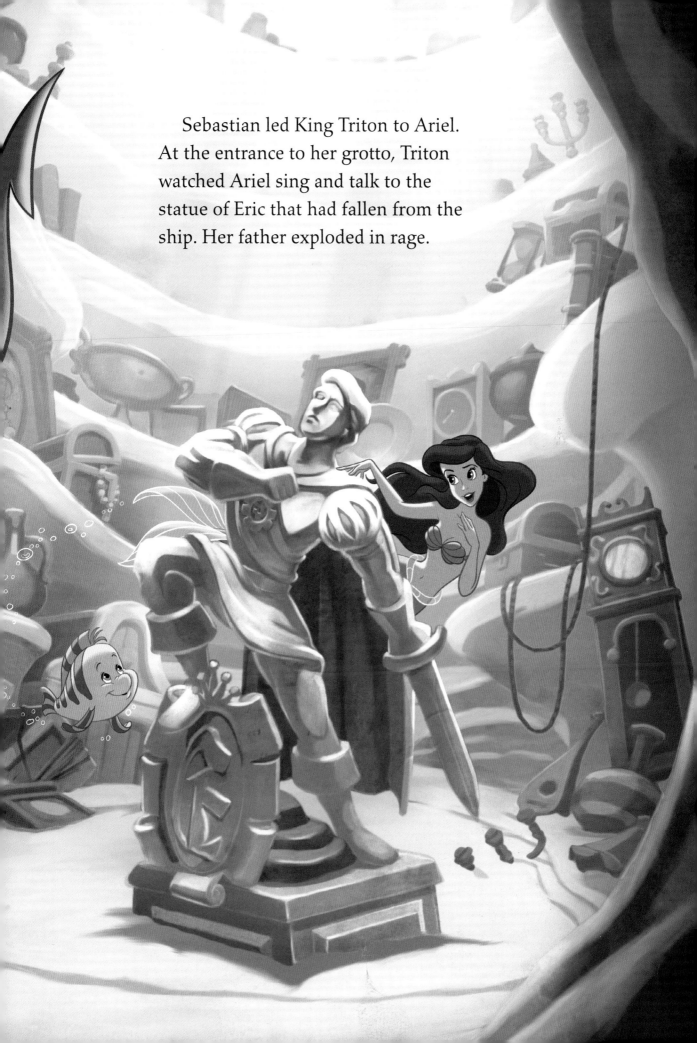

"Contact between the human world and the merworld is strictly forbidden!" he thundered.

But Ariel wouldn't give in. "Daddy, I love him," she said.

"I am going to get through to you. And if this is the only way, so be it!" Triton shouted, raising his trident. Flashes of light filled the room. In moments, Eric's statue and the rest of Ariel's treasures were shattered.

As Ariel sobbed among the ruins, Flotsam and Jetsam, Ursula's pet eels, slithered out from the shadows.

"Poor, sweet child," they hissed. "The sea witch can help you. She can make all your dreams come true."

Although Ariel feared the sea
witch, she followed the eels. Pale
creatures gazed at Ariel with
hopeless eyes as she approached
Ursula's cavern.

"Come in," Ursula coaxed with a
cruel smile.

Ursula offered to turn Ariel into a human for a price—her voice. But there was one catch: Eric had to kiss her before sunset on the third day.

"If he doesn't, you turn back into a mermaid, and you belong to me!" Ursula cackled.

I hereby grant unto URSULA, the Witch of the Sea, one voice, in exchange for tyon once high. Dinu egihn thon zibzo serr'n Phur-gurr'i rehi frasi retn r'm scire urph'm srcrp munk gurck, Ch Lich noy ri imm. To mund

for all eternity.
signed,

Frightened but determined, Ariel
signed the glowing contract.
"Now sing," Ursula commanded.
As Ariel's voice flowed from her,
Ursula captured it in a seashell.

The sea churned around the mermaid. Suddenly,
her tail disappeared. In its place, she found two legs.
Now that Ariel was human, she couldn't live underwater.
Quickly, Flounder and Sebastian rushed her to the surface.

Ariel was delighted with her new legs, but Sebastian was worried. Should he tell King Triton? Sebastian knew Ariel would be miserable without Eric, so he promised to help her, as did Flounder and Scuttle.

"If you wanna be a human, the first thing you gotta do is dress like one," Scuttle explained. He and Sebastian wrapped Ariel in a ragged old sail.

Just then, Eric's dog, Max, bounded across the beach, and Eric chased after him.

"You seem very familiar to me," Eric told Ariel.
He studied her face. Was she the girl with the
beautiful voice who had rescued him? But when Eric
realized Ariel couldn't speak, his hopes were crushed.
She couldn't be the girl he sought.

Eric took Ariel to his palace,
where his friendly servants cared
for her. He couldn't believe how
beautiful she looked when she
appeared in the great hall cleaned up
and dressed in a lovely gown.

At the dinner table, Sebastian hid on Ariel's platter. Grimsby and Eric didn't notice. They were watching Ariel comb her hair with a fork. Grimsby was surprised, but Eric thought Ariel was charming.

The next day, Prince Eric showed
Ariel his kingdom. She smelled
flowers, tasted human food, and
danced for the first time. Eric's world
was wonderful, and now she was part
of it. But he still had not kissed her,
and there was only one day left!

As the sun set, Eric took Ariel rowing in a lagoon.
While they floated, Sebastian—with the help of the
other creatures—orchestrated a love song. Prince Eric
gazed at Ariel. He leaned closer . . . closer . . . their lips
almost touching when . . .

SPLASH! Flotsam and Jetsam tipped the boat, toppling Eric and Ariel into the water.

Ursula watched from her cavern. "That was too close," she said. "It's time I took matters into my own tentacles." She transformed herself into a beautiful girl named Vanessa.

Eric wondered if he'd ever find the mysterious girl with the beautiful voice. Vanessa appeared on the beach, wearing a necklace that contained Ariel's voice. When he saw Vanessa and heard her singing, he instantly fell under her spell.

"Wake up!" Scuttle flew into Ariel's room the next morning. "Congratulations, kiddo, we did it! Eric's getting married today."

Ariel's heart filled with joy. Eric was in love with her! It was too wonderful to be true!

But Eric wasn't marrying Ariel. He was marrying Vanessa. Ariel's heart ached. She had lost her true love, and now she would never escape Ursula's clutches.

Once aboard the ship, the sea witch gloated. Her plan was working beautifully. Soon she would rule the seas. Ursula didn't notice Scuttle peeking through a porthole or hear him gasp when he saw her true reflection in the mirror. He flew back to tell Ariel.

Ariel and her friends had to stop the wedding! Ariel clung to a barrel while Flounder towed her toward the ship, and Sebastian raced to find King Triton. But the sun was going down. They had to move fast!

The wedding had already started when Flounder and Ariel arrived at the ship. Eric stood in a trance before the minister. His eyes were dull and glazed, and Vanessa slyly smirked, happy that all had gone according to her plan. She was sure she had won!

But before Vanessa could say her vows, all the animals that Scuttle had rounded up came to the rescue. A flock of bluebirds swooped down, pecking Vanessa and yanking her hair while pelicans, seals, starfish, and dolphins joined the attack.

"Get away from me, you slimy little . . ." Vanessa screamed as Scuttle yanked off her shell necklace. It flew through the air and shattered on the deck. Ariel's voice flowed back to her.

"Eric!" she said at last.

Eric was released from the spell. "You're the one!" he exclaimed, looking at Ariel. "It was you all the time."

"Get away from her!" Vanessa screamed.

Before Prince Eric could kiss Ariel, the sun sank beneath the horizon.

"You're too late!" Vanessa shouted as Ariel became a mermaid again. With a flash of lightning, Vanessa transformed back into Ursula and dragged Ariel into the sea. Eric went after Ariel.

"I'm not gonna lose her again!" he shouted.

Suddenly, King Triton appeared, brandishing his trident. "Ursula! Let her go!"

"She's mine now," Ursula replied, showing him Ariel's contract. "We made a deal. Of course, I might be willing to make an exchange."

To save his beloved daughter, King Triton agreed to take Ariel's place. Now he would be Ursula's servant forever. Ariel watched, horrified, as her father began to shrivel away.

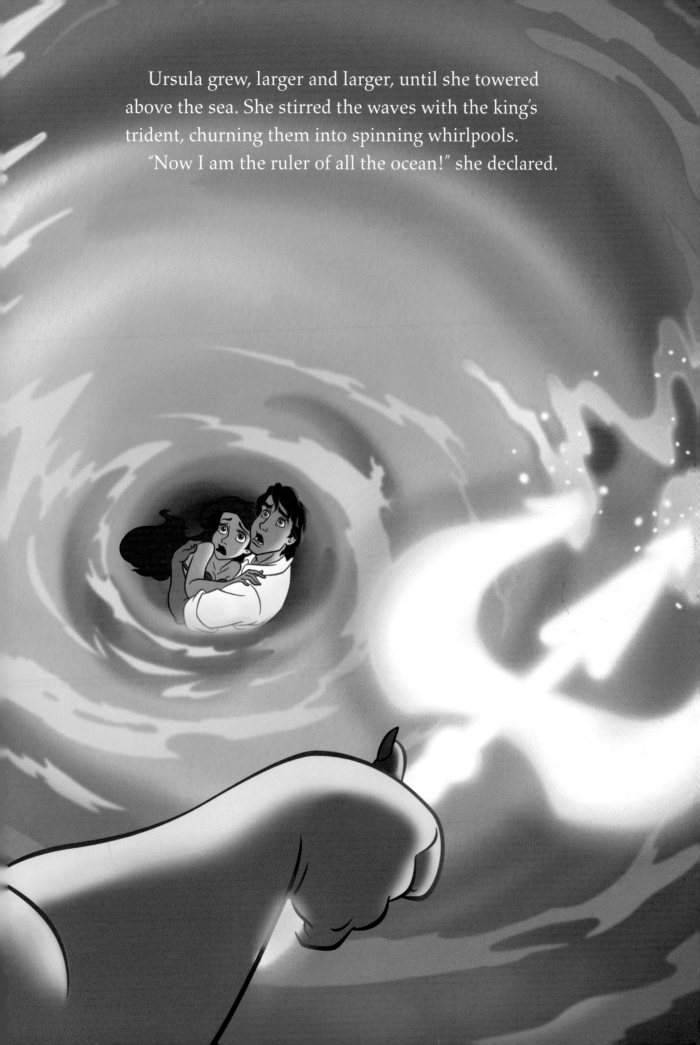

Ursula grew, larger and larger, until she towered above the sea. She stirred the waves with the king's trident, churning them into spinning whirlpools. "Now I am the ruler of all the ocean!" she declared.

"Say good-bye to your sweetheart!" Ursula shouted, aiming fiery bolts at Eric.

But he didn't give up. Just then, he saw an ancient sunken ship rising through a whirlpool. He clambered aboard and steered its jagged bow through Ursula's heart.

With a howl, the sea witch disappeared beneath the waves. Her spell was broken. Her curse over the merfolk had ended. King Triton and all the poor unfortunate souls she had held prisoner were free at last.

But Ariel was still a mermaid. And Eric would always be a human. King Triton watched his daughter gaze longingly toward the shore and the man she loved.

With a sigh, he touched his trident to the water, and Ariel became human once again.

King Triton smiled as he watched
Ariel reunite with Prince Eric.

Ariel's friends and family cheered on the day Ariel and Prince Eric got married. At last she was part of the human world she loved. And she would live there happily ever after.

To be continued . . .